Good-bye, Havana!

Hola, New York!

EDIE COLÓN   Illustrated by RAÚL COLÓN

A PAULA WISEMAN BOOK
SIMON & SCHUSTER BOOKS FOR YOUNG READERS
NEW YORK   LONDON   TORONTO   SYDNEY

In loving memory of my grandpa "Abito" Carlos Valdes and my grandma
"Abuelita" Esther San Pedro, who are both missed dearly, and in recognition
of my parents for having experienced such difficult times to better my life
—E. C.

To the immigrant spirit, the lifeblood of great nations
—R. C.

SIMON & SCHUSTER BOOKS FOR YOUNG READERS • An imprint of Simon & Schuster Children's Publishing Division • 1230 Avenue of the Americas, New York, New York 10020 • Text copyright © 2011 by Edie Colón • Illustrations copyright © 2011 by Raúl Colón • All rights reserved, including the right of reproduction in whole or in part in any form. • SIMON & SCHUSTER BOOKS FOR YOUNG READERS is a trademark of Simon & Schuster, Inc. • Book design by Laurent Linn • The text for this book is set in Fairfield LT Std. • The illustrations for this book are rendered in watercolor, colored pencils, and lithograph pencils. • Manufactured in China • 0716 SCP • 2 4 6 8 10 9 7 5 3 • Library of Congress Cataloging-in-Publication Data • Colón, Edie. • Good-bye, Havana! Hola, New York! / Edie Colón ; illustrated by Raúl Colón. • p. cm. • "A Paula Wiseman Book." • Summary: When Fidel Castro's government takes over their restaurant in 1960, six-year-old Gabriella and her parents move from Cuba to New York City. • ISBN 978-1-4424-0674-2 (hardcover) 1. Cuban Americans—Juvenile fiction. [1. Cuban Americans—Fiction. 2. Immigrants—Fiction. 3. Emigration and immigration—Fiction. 4. Cuba—History—1959–1990—Fiction. 5. Bronx (New York, N.Y.)—History—20th century—Fiction.] I. Colón, Raúl, ill. II. Title. • PZ7.C71632Goo 2011 • [E]—dc22 • 2010020932 • ISBN 978-1-4424-3484-4 (eBook)

GABRIELLA WOKE UP EARLY. It was a warm and sunny November day.
She could hear the sounds of the beach, especially the waves that sounded
like they were making music through her window.

For the last few weeks Mother and Father had not been home. Gabriella's *mami* had told her that they were going on a trip and would be back soon. She didn't say how long they'd be gone. Gabriella hoped they would call soon. It was lonely without them. Gabriella was staying with her *abuelita*—grandma—and her *abuelito*—grandpa—whom she had nicknamed Abito.

That morning Abuelita said to Gabriella, "*Hoy vas a ir a un nuevo país, los Estados Unidos, para vivir con Mami y Papi.* Today you are going to a new country, the United States, where you will live with Mami and Papi."

Gabriella felt confused. "*Por qué tengo que irme?* Why do I have to go?"

Abito explained, "*En los Estados Unidos tendrás una vida mejor.* You will have a better life in the United States."

Abuelita said, "*Gabriella, hay muchos problemas en Cuba.* Gabriella, there are many problems in Cuba."

Gabriella had heard her parents talking about something called a revolution. She remembered her *abito* and *papi* talking about a man named Fidel Castro, the president of Cuba. She heard them say that Castro had taken Cuba over by force. Everything seemed different to Gabriella since Castro had become the new president. Last week, from inside her house, she could hear some people screaming on the street, "Fidel! Fidel!" Some of them seemed happy and others seemed angry.

Gabriella heard her parents say that her friend Ana's father had been taken away one night while Ana slept. Ana couldn't go visit him. The grown-ups said that he had helped something called the Resistance. Gabriella knew that things weren't like they had been before. At home she saw that Abito and Abuelita were not going to work anymore. The government had closed their restaurant. She heard Abito saying that Castro and his government had the power to take away the people's freedom and everything they owned.

That afternoon Gabriella's grandparents took her to the airport. Her *papi* was waiting for them there. Gabriella was so happy to see Papi, and he was happy to see her. Papi hugged Gabriella and said, "*Por fin mi hija, estamos juntos.* Finally, my daughter, we are together." Papi looked serious as he spoke to Abuelita and Abito, and Gabriella wondered where Mami was. Abuelita and Abito said good-bye to Gabriella. She thought she saw Abuelita and Abito crying from the plane window, but she wasn't sure. It felt good the way Papi held her hand tight.

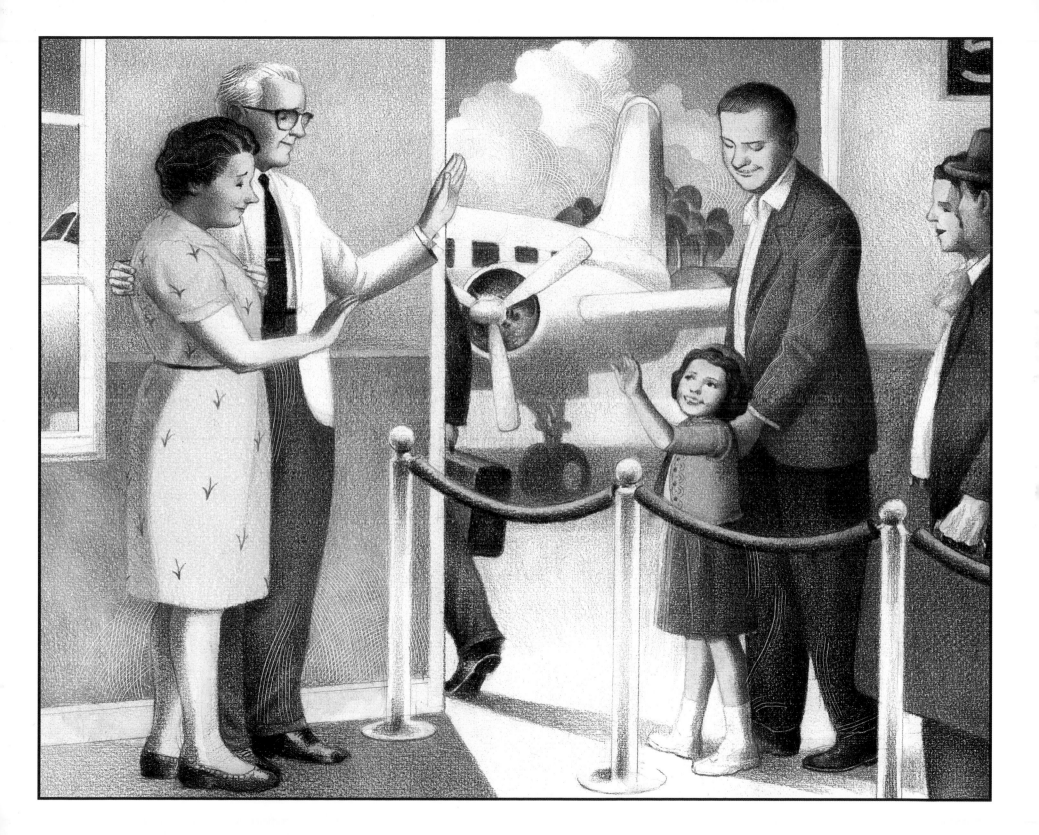

As the plane was landing, Gabriella looked out the window and saw huge, tall buildings. To her, the buildings looked like the castles she had seen in the books Abuelita read to her. At the airport her *mami* and her other grandma and grandpa were waiting for her. Gabriella walked off the airplane and ran into Mami's arms.

"*Hola, Mami! Estoy tan contenta de verte.* Hello, Mami! I am so happy to see you. *Dónde vamos ahora?* Where are we going now?"

Mami smiled and said, "*A nuestra nueva casa.* To our new house."

They all hugged and kissed Gabriella.

Grandma Frida gave Gabriella a beautiful tall doll and told her, "*Bienvenida a los Estados Unidos. Ésta es tu nueva amiga, Penny.* Welcome to America. This is your new friend, Penny." Gabriella was surprised that Penny wore a sweater, heavy pants, a large jacket, and boots. Gabriella was used to wearing shorts and going barefoot. Grandpa Morris explained that here in New York it was cold in winter, unlike Cuba.

The next day, when Gabriella awoke in her own room in a new home, she noticed a family picture on her dresser. The picture helped Gabriella feel a little better. Her new house in the Bronx was not as big as her house in Cuba. She could not hear the waves or see the beach. She heard many cars and trucks outside her window. The cars and trucks were covered with snow. Gabriella had never seen snow before. She missed her toys, the sound of the beach, and Abuelita and Abito.

That morning she asked her *mami*, "A qué hora *viene Abito hoy para llevarme al parque?* When is Abito picking me up today to take me to the park?" Gabriella couldn't understand why Mami started to cry. Mami told her that Abito and Abuelita were far away. Mami explained that Gabriella would have to draw them pictures and send them by mail for now.

That Saturday night after dinner Papi explained to Gabriella that she would start a new school the day after tomorrow. She was going to school to learn how to speak English. How was she going to understand her teacher and all the children? Gabriella wondered. For the first time since she arrived to America, Gabriella felt afraid.

On Gabriella's first day of school Mami brought her to her classroom. Gabriella felt very worried. She whispered to Mami, *"No me dejes aquí sola. Quédate conmigo.* Don't leave me alone here. Stay with me."

Mami held Gabriella's hand and very seriously said to her, *"La maestra y los niños te ayudarán.* The teacher and the children will help you." The teacher, Miss Lepoor, asked Mami to wave good-bye.

There were many new faces. Miss Lepoor kept talking to Gabriella, but Gabriella did not understand. She started to cry. Miss Lepoor used her hands to show that she wanted Gabriella to sit down. Even though Gabriella couldn't yet talk to Miss Lepoor, she could tell from her eyes that she was nice.

During that first day Gabriella just listened to the children and the teacher speaking in English, but she did not understand. Gabriella played with the dolls by herself. She wished she had her friend Penny at school with her. She would ask if she could bring her tomorrow. That afternoon when Mami picked her up, Gabriella gave her a drawing of her new school that she had made for Abuelita and Abito. Mami said she would mail it to them.

Gabriella liked her music teacher, Mrs. Humphrey. Mrs. Humphrey taught the children songs that had Spanish words. Gabriella's favorites were all of the Christmas songs, especially "Noche de paz," which was "Silent Night" in Spanish. Mrs. Humphrey would ask Gabriella to help her say the words.

During the next few months school became easier. Gabriella learned many new words and phrases, such as "hello," "good-bye," "please," "thank you," "I like," "I don't like," "yes," and "no." She had one friend named Alan who played with her on the swings and helped her paint. Although they couldn't talk to each other a lot, they still played together and smiled at each other. As time went on, Gabriella learned more and more English words.

Gabriella loved lunch time because of the hot lunches served. She was learning to eat many new American foods, like macaroni and cheese, meatloaf, and hot dogs. She liked them all, especially the hot dogs. After lunch, Gabriella liked playtime best. She practiced teaching her dolls how to speak English.

Soon it was spring. Mami was excited because she said that they were going to be able to speak to Abuelita and Abito on the telephone. They had not spoken in five months because President Castro had decided you had to wait your turn to call Cuba from America. Gabriella had had a long wait. A telephone operator connected them: "Person-to-person for Mr. Valdes." Gabriella was so excited to hear her grandparents' voices.

She told them about her new school and about her best friends, Alan and Penny. She told them she was eating new foods. She told them that in America you had to wear different clothes during different seasons—winter, spring, summer, and fall. Before she could say good-bye, the operator interrupted the call. Gabriella couldn't hear Abito and Abuelita anymore. Once again Mami cried. Gabriella missed them so much, but she didn't say so because she knew it would make Mami even sadder.

By June, Gabriella was able to speak English well. She had made more friends—Donna, Judy, and David—although Penny and Alan were still her favorites. One day when Gabriella came home from school, Mami and Papi had good news. Abuelita would be coming to America.

Gabriella was so excited! She had not seen Abuelita for so many months. "Why isn't Abito coming too?" she asked. Papi explained that only a certain number of people could leave Cuba at a time. Abito would come too, in just two months, Papi promised her. It was Abuelita's turn, not Abito's turn yet.

The day finally arrived: August 20, 1960. Abuelita was coming to America. Mami, Papi, and Gabriella went to the airport to pick her up. They waited by the airport gate, watching many people get off the plane. For the longest time they did not see her. The last person to get off the plane was Abuelita. Mami and Papi cried happy tears. Gabriella knew what would make Abuelita happy. She ran into Abuelita's arms. She had a surprise for Abuelita. "Welcome to America," Gabriella said. She gave Abuelita a packet of gum. "This is for you, Abuelita, because in America we chew gum, and I am your new friend in America."

The Bronx was cold in the winter and there were cars, not an ocean, outside the window, but two months later when Abito arrived, they were a family again.

The Bronx was Gabriella's new home, *su nuevo hogar*.

Spanish Words

Abito: Gabriella's nickname for
  her grandfather
abuela: grandmother
abuelita: grandma
abuelito: grandpa
abuelo: grandfather
ahora: now
amiga: friend (female)
amigo: friend (male)
aquí: here

bienvenidos: welcome
casa: house
contenta, contento: happy
Estados Unidos: United States
hogar: home
hoy: today
juntos: together
maestra: teacher (female)
maestro: teacher (male)
mami: mommy

mi hija: my daughter
mi hijo: my son
muchos: many
niñas: girls
niños: children or boys
nuevo, nueva: new
papi: daddy
problemas: problems
vida: life
vivir: to live

Author's Note

The story in *Good-bye, Havana! Hola, New York!* is inspired by my childhood in Cuba and New York as best as I can remember. I asked my mother and father for their help in gathering the facts for this story, as parents often remember more than their children do. I gave the main character the name Gabriella so that I could have some distance from my story, although the events in this book all happened and they happened to me.

I remember my grandfather Carlos talking with my grandma Esther about a man called Fulgencio Batista. He was the president of Cuba at the time that another man named Fidel Castro was trying to take over Cuba. Many people were saying that Batista was the best person for Cuba, but some adults were saying that the best thing for the country was for Batista to leave and for Castro, the leader of the revolution, to take over the presidency.

In the early morning hours of January 1, 1959, while the country was celebrating the arrival of the new year, a rumor spread like wildfire that President Batista had left the country. We eventually found out the rumor was true: President Fulgencio Batista had boarded a plane and left Cuba. Fidel Castro and his men had taken possession of Cuba.

Thousands and thousands of people came out onto the streets of Havana and started singing and screaming, "Fidel! Fidel!" Because Batista had left without any notice, there was no security on the streets. Many civilians took charge of policing the streets and remained in place until Castro's army took charge.

Castro had won the revolution. Castro and his men were received with great happiness by the majority of Cubans. At first, to many Cuban people, Castro was a savior. They wanted change.

In his new role Castro gave long speeches about the new reforms of the country. During one of his famous speeches he declared that he was a Communist. Slowly he began confiscating companies, banks, and businesses. The government took over everything, including the restaurant my parents and grandparents owned. That was when my mother and father went to New York. It took my family one year and seven months to be together again. I have set the story in 1960, when I first came to New York.